THE TURNED GODS SERIES
CHARACTER COMPANION

LILLY'S GAME

JOYCE SERRANO

INTRODUCTION

Lilly's Game is the introduction of Lilly into The Turned Gods book series. The time frame of this character background piece is after Book 1 - Original Grace and before Book 2 - Immortals In The Everything.

CHAPTER ONE

This was exactly what Lilly had imagined a black site interrogation chamber would look like: cold concrete, no windows, shitty lighting. Static noise assaulted her ears from headphones strapped in place. She still couldn't figure out how the hell they had caught her. She twisted as much as the bindings would allow, cracking her neck. Her head throbbed dully, and her senses were clouded. She was both pissed and confused.

She could feel crusted blood on her mouth, from biting through her lip when her face hit the ground. They got her with something good. Blinking through her clouded vision, Lilly wondered how long she had been bound to the cold metal chair. She pulled against carbon fiber ankle straps, leg straps, one across her waist, another across her chest, with no sign of give.

"Shit!" she exclaimed as shackles bit deep into her wrist when she tried to wipe her mouth. Fresh blood dripped onto the table in front of her. Each hand had been chained far enough apart she couldn't make them touch. The chair and table were unmovable, anchored into the concrete floor. The only weak spot she could see was the door and nobody in their right mind could say that was weak. Steel covered the exterior, with no internal handle or hinges. No control pads. No visible way out. There weren't any viewing mirrors, but someone was clearly watching her. You didn't leave a girl like Lilly unattended even if she was restrained. Whoever it was, they certainly weren't playing around. Even she wouldn't be able to get out of this mess on wits alone.

She should have known the money was too good to be true. It made her look past the risk. After all, no one had ever even come close to catching her before. Much less, blindside her the way these people had. She still had no idea where she had gone wrong. Her brain was moving too slowly to be accurate which was most frustrating as she tried to go through every step. She had used multiple proxies, ran through back servers, no alarms, no breadcrumbs. File download was flawless. She hadn't even signed this hack. The job specs had come through an alias profile on the dark web. Neither hers, nor the buyer's identities were traceable. Even her internet connection was a masked IP over a citywide, public network.

"Somebody want to tell me what the hell is going on here?!" she yelled out aggressively.

A guard joked to his partner as they watched the monitor at the other end of a long hallway. "We'll be right in, sweetheart."

The door opened behind the two men while they were still laughing. A tall, slender woman with short, dark hair entered the room. Her eyes were cold, nearly as black as her hair. Her cheekbones sat high, smoothly sliding into a slender jawline carrying full lips. She was a classic, Italian beauty, dressed in a light pink fitted designer suit. Under the suit jacket was a crisp white, high-collar shirt buttoned to the top. She wore dark pink pumps and carried a leather satchel dyed in the same hue as her outfit. She tossed the bag on the end of the table beside the guard on the right. Standing behind the men, she leaned forward, resting one hand on the back of each chair.

"You think that might be a little overkill?" she said in a cold tone. It wasn't meant to be a question.

"No," said the man on the right. "You didn't see how many darts we had to hit her with to take her down." His tone was condescending, and she immediately dubbed him 'Jackass One.'

The second man in the room glanced at the woman dismissively. "I thought he was sending Grace." His attitude earned him the moniker of 'Jackass Two.'

"Grace is a little busy. You got me. Is there a problem with that?" Vivienne didn't want to be there any more than they wanted her there. She was in the middle of planning a wedding and a turning, straddled between two planets. She didn't have time to waste on this. Ivan had to think it was important. He didn't ask favors often, so when the Regent asked you to do something, you dropped everything and went.

"No, ma'am. No problem," Jackass Two answered. What could Ivan have been thinking of sending someone barely over one hundred to face off with a devious and manipulative deserter, possessing nearly a thousand years of experience over Vivienne?

Many vampires still held animosity toward Lilly and a few others. After the vampire exterminations, the community was left scattered and crippled. At a time when they needed to come together to survive, Lilly and some others had abandoned them. She isolated herself, lived alone on the fringes, neither in the vampire world, nor the human one. And now, if word of what she had done were to get out, some of those within the community would be calling for her life. Maybe that was entirely the reason Ivan had sent Vivienne. Vivienne hadn't been alive for the near extinction. She harbored no animosity toward this woman and was empathetic without being emotional. She was pragmatic, unhindered by feelings of resentment.

Vivienne studied the girl on the monitor. Lilly was a bit under average height for a female. Average, slender build for a young woman from the time she was turned. The oversized clothing she wore did its job hiding her figure. Her hair was dyed black, braided down both sides of her head. It was difficult to tell what her exact ethnicity was. She looked like a mix of Asian and European, possibly a Pacific Islander. Her eyes were more rounded than almond shaped. Her skin, a light tan color and flawless except for the current wounds. She looked like a scared, defensive child. Had she even been of turning age? She couldn't have been much older than sixteen at the time.

"I didn't expect her to be so …" Vivienne trailed off.

"Young?" Jackass One snorted.

"Delicate." Vivienne shot him a hard look.

"Don't let her innocent looks deceive you. She's as feral as they come. It took five darts to take her down and she still managed to break my arm," Jackass Two added.

"I think I'd act like a wild animal too if someone had come after me like that." Vivienne wasn't interested in their opinions. "You were supposed to bring her in quietly."

She pulled a laptop, a large metal water bottle, and a small flash style device out of her bag. When she turned to leave the room, Jackass One got up and reached for the doorknob. Vivienne placed her hand against the door and held it shut. She turned her head, looking at the guard over her shoulder.

"Thank you, but I should go on my own. I'll get more out of her if she doesn't feel threatened."

"I'm not so sure Ivan would want us to leave you alone in there with her."

"I think Ivan sent me because he trusts my judgment. I mean, that's assuming he didn't ask you to talk to her first. Did he? I mean, I'm sure he explained what was going on to you before he called me, right? … No?" Vivienne could be cutting when she was irritated and everything about this situation irritated her. She also wasn't a fan of having her authority challenged.

Jackass One scoffed at her, releasing the doorknob. "Well then … if that's how you want it. Just scream if you need anything. We'll try to make it in there before she bleeds you out."

Vivienne yanked the door open, mumbling under her breath as she walked down the hall. "I'm sure you'll be in right quick, won't you?" Those two would be more than happy to have an excuse to kill Lilly, even if it meant Vivienne being critically injured.

Lilly looked up when the door opened. Aw, shit, she thought, as the familiar low vibration of being near another vampire coursed through her. It would have been so much better if it had been humans that caught her. Why were vampires coming after her? She tried to stay off their radar. She hadn't interacted with more than a handful of them in centuries. Most of the ones she did have contact with were like her, on the fringes.

"It took you long enough," Lilly sneered.

Vivienne saw the look of disdain on Lilly's face. She crossed the room, pulling Lilly's headphones off before she placed her hand on the wall, activating a digital panel to turn off the cameras and the sound. She tossed the laptop and flash device onto the table, knowing it would get Lilly's attention; curiosity would hold it.

"Awesome. Here I am trussed up like a calf at a cattle roping competition and lucky me I get stuck with ditsy in pink for an interrogator."

"If you think you could behave yourself long enough to have an adult conversation, I'll remove the shackles from your wrists."

"And if I can't?" she smirked.

Vivienne walked around to sit in the chair across from Lilly. She folded her hands on the table in front of her and stared blankly into Lilly's unwavering eyes. It was a power move. Vivienne could sit there all day. The girl would now need to ask to be let loose. Vivienne wouldn't make the offer again, but she hadn't rescinded it either.

Lilly did want the shackles off. Her choices were either give in and ask to be released or continue to be a stubborn ass and remain restrained. Stuff my fucking pride, she thought to herself. It's not like it had ever done her any good before. What was Ditsy going to do to her anyway? Brush her hair? She looked like the hardest day she'd ever had was a catastrophic broken nail.

Lilly cleared her throat. "I would appreciate having the shackles removed." She smiled clenching her jaw like the words tasted bitter.

"Pleeease," she added. "I would also appreciate knowing why, exactly, am I here?"

Vivienne rose silently walking back to the panel to unlock Lilly's hands. Lilly rubbed her wrists, feeling the small cuts and bruises heal themselves. Vivienne crossed back around the table taking her seat again.

"Let's start with something a little simpler. I am Vivienne. Would you like a drink?" Vivienne opened the water bottle, tipping it toward Lilly.

Lilly sniffed. It wasn't blood. It wasn't water either. It smelled heavy, metallic, like food. "You first," she answered distrustfully.

Vivienne took a swig passing the bottle back to Lilly. She took a tentative sip swirling it around her mouth before swallowing. Then she downed the rest of the bottle. The cool liquid felt soothing on her swollen throat and tongue.

"What is this?" Lilly asked. It was probably a question she should have considered before downing the entire bottle.

"CB. Oh Lilly, don't tell me you're still drinking human blood. You have no idea how far our technology has come in the last half century, do you?" Vivienne could tell Lilly was proud of being smart. She wanted to make her feel stupid, like she was being left behind the rest of her race. Although she had done her research, Vivienne didn't know Lilly's story, other than early on she flitted from clan to clan, not sticking around long enough to gain attachments. The last few hundred years, she was totally isolated. No one knew Lilly's background or sire line.

Lilly curled her lip and clenched her jaw. Was this woman toying with her? She'd heard rumors for the last century about creating a blood replacement. Had they finally done it or was this some kind of trick?

"I don't kill humans," Lilly snarled, hardening her features. Except for that once, before I understood. The guilt riddled thought smoldered at the back of her mind. She locked eyes with Vivienne.

Vivienne didn't break eye contact, though she did backpedal slightly.

"I didn't accuse you of being a murderer. I accused you of being disengaged from the community." She pulled a card out of the inside pocket of her blazer and slid it across the table. "Here. CB is free to all vampires. Call that number anytime and it will be delivered to you wherever you are. You never need to worry how to quench your thirst or being caught for doing so."

Lilly scanned the room, landing her eyes back on Vivienne. "That's so helpful to me in here," she replied doubting she would ever be leaving this room. "Nothing is really free, Vivienne. What's the catch?" Lilly was suspicious. Years on the outside had made her cynical.

"The only tradeoff is you don't kill humans. Since you say you don't anyway, then for you it is free, isn't it?" Vivienne took a breath. She didn't want to appear angry. This woman didn't trust them. She didn't trust any authority. Whether Lilly had reason or not, Vivienne needed to keep her open and talking. "We don't want attention drawn toward the community. We don't want humans to start hunting us again, not even you. You are still part of this community whether you believe you are or not. You put yourself on the outside. We didn't do that to you."

"Yeah, if that's true, then why am I sitting here tied to a chair?"

"Because you've done something that could cause us harm. And I don't think you'd have come to answer questions if we'd have said 'pretty please'."

"So, you're the one who put me in this chair?" Lilly asked snidely.

"No, I'm not the one who put you there. I'm the one who can let you out." Vivienne matched Lilly's tone.

Lilly leaned her head to one side. "Hm, so, you drew the short straw."

"It appears so."

"Well then, let's get on with it. How do I earn my way out?" Lilly slouched as much as she could, slinging one arm over the back of her chair.

"Who hired you to get the list? Why would you come after that?" Vivienne leaned back, relaxing her stiff posture slightly.

"Who? No idea. I don't work for a 'who.' I work for a 'what.' And the 'what' is money. I don't care who they are; I don't care what they want. If they can pay, I get it." Lilly shrugged.

"What if it's something they shouldn't have?"

"Who are you to say what someone should or shouldn't have?" Lilly leaned forward folding her arms. Her lips curled. Vivienne had struck a nerve.

"What if it's a list of every vampire on the planet including you? Worried about who should and shouldn't have that?" Vivienne leaned forward again, with cold eyes and an unflinching face.

Lilly deflated. "Fuck."

"Good thing you weren't able to complete the hack," Vivienne said calmly.

"I did complete the hack. I downloaded the file." Lilly's attitude hadn't diminished.

"Mmm." Vivienne made a small facial shrug. "You downloaded a file. Do you think we're stupid enough to leave the real list on a network server?"

Lilly swiftly went from smug to irritated. "If it wasn't the file, what am I doing here?"

"Because when whoever got those names starts killing people and realizes they're just regular humans, guess who they're coming after next?"

"Isn't that rich. You put out a list of innocent humans to be murdered and because you didn't kill them yourself it's supposed to be okay? And then you justify using me as bait to catch the humans killing them, thinking they're us? Why didn't you just make it harder to get the list?" Lilly's irritation was turning to anger.

"Would you have stopped? Would another hacker have stopped? It was a challenge. It was a game for you. And the people on that list are far from innocent."

"Judge and jury now, are you?"

"I'm not the one who set this all into motion. Most of the names on that list are fictitious. Some are deceased. Some are names our people have used in past lives. A few," Vivienne leaned forward, "are active serial killers that will never be caught because they go from country to country, killing one or two before moving on. Human authorities will not connect the dots, because they don't talk to each other. We consider it a public service."

"Oh, so they are vampires then." Lilly jeered at Vivienne, disgusted at her apparent justification, protecting an entire race of killers by giving up a few human ones.

"No, Lilly. They're monsters. When our race used to kill, before we realized we could feed without taking a life, it was for food. These humans kill each other for pleasure. One human on the list keeps a finger from each child he rapes and murders. Another, kidnaps their victims, torturing them for months before eventually starving them to death. Do you know what a horrible death starvation is? Let's not take into consideration the broken bones, or hooks through their skin …"

Lilly cut her off, raising her hands in front of her. "That's enough. I get your point. What do you want from me?"

"From where I'm sitting Lilly, this has two ways it can go. Either you can be seen as the one who sold us out or you can be the one helping us find whoever is hunting us down. Your choice."

"I didn't sell us out," Lilly defended.

"You didn't know you weren't selling us out when you stole the list. It's about perception anyway, not facts, isn't it? Are you going to help or not?"

"What happens if I don't?"

"Nothing. If you don't want to help, we're not going force you. We let you go. People die. Your new friends come to find you. We didn't have to pick you up at all, Lilly. We could have let this play out. You never would have known they were coming for you. We haven't lost anything out of this exchange." Vivienne stood up and walked around behind Lilly making a gesture on the wall panel releasing the rest of her restraints.

"All we need is for you to get us to the place where you found whoever it was that hired you. We'll do the rest. Or you can get up and walk out of here." Vivienne shoved the laptop in front of Lilly, then went back to her seat. She hoped the illusion of being in control would be enough to keep Lilly from coming after her across the table. She was relying on her instinct that Lilly didn't want to hurt her. If she had wanted to, there would be nothing Vivienne could do about it. She knew she was outmatched in both speed and strength.

CHAPTER TWO

Lilly placed her elbows on the table resting her chin on her folded hands scrutinizing Vivienne, who didn't flinch.

"I found this gig on the dark web. You're not going to be able to track this guy." Lilly hadn't moved and didn't touch the laptop.

"Let us worry about that." Vivienne shoved the laptop closer to Lilly, relieved she had chosen to talk and not attack. "What makes you think it's one guy?"

Lilly glanced at the laptop, then looked back at Vivienne. It wasn't a question she had expected or had thought about. "I don't know. The tone of the way it was written. The writer used masculine terms. The sentences were short, succinct, and abrupt. There weren't any sensory terms. They always wrote 'I' not 'we'. Then again, males tend to do that even if it is a group. Taking singular credit, saying things like 'I want this', or 'my idea'. It could be a group, although I believe the person I was in contact with was male."

"What did they tell you they were looking for? What made you target that specific list?" Vivienne continued regaining her confidence.

"They didn't give me anything specific. All I knew was it was a list of names with some personal data. It would have been assembled within the last year and kept current. I started with file types that could be used in a database. They said it was a few thousand names, just text, so I estimated the larger file sizes and narrowed it down to around twenty files that fit the criteria. The final piece in selecting that specific file was the consistency of the updates. It was updated at least twice a week, every week, for the last ten months. Other files of the same type were seldom touched. You went to a lot of trouble to make this particular file appealing."

"That was the point, wasn't it?"

"I guess it was." Lilly raised her eyebrows as she reached out, opening the laptop. It was thick and lighter than she expected for its size. Then she realized it wasn't a laptop at all, only a case. Inside was a small device that resembled a pack of gum pushed into foam packing. She picked it up and examined it closely. It was solid, smooth, and cold, resembling metal, only much lighter.

"What am I supposed to do with this?" Lilly held it up in front of her pushing the laptop-looking case to the side.

"There's nothing you can do with it until we code you in. I told you, Lilly. We've come a long way with technology. That little TAC makes the supercharged system you're working with look like a relic."

"TAC?" Lilly asked.

"It's an acronym for a language I don't speak. The device itself scans and connects to any communication protocol. Microwave, cellular, Wi-Fi, NFC, telepathic. You name it, it can connect to it."

"Yeah, right," Lilly replied, sarcastically.

Vivienne picked up the digital flash and slipped off the cover. It had a flat clear end resembling a slice of opalescent crystal. She reached for Lilly's mouth, but Lilly dodged her grasp.

"I need a venom sample." Vivienne put one hand on her hip, holding the device in the other.

"You could have asked." Lilly raised her lip letting her canis descend.

"My fault. I'm used to our tech and people who understand what's going on." Vivienne replied maintaining her 'in charge' persona. She pressed the device against Lilly's fang, taking a single drop of venom.

Vivienne took the device from Lilly and pressed the crystal against it. A slot opened absorbing the crystal, and she handed it back to Lilly.

"There you go. You have access to all our devices. With narrowly limited privileges, of course."

"Of course," Lilly mirrored. "How do I make it work?"

"Place a finger on each end and click it."

Lilly did as she was instructed. The device opened to the size of a large smart phone or small tablet. The metal she had been holding became the bottom part of the frame with the screen displayed in the air above. Only it wasn't a simple hologram. It was tactile.

"If that's not large enough, pull the corners and drag it open."

"How big can it get?" Lilly was excited by the device almost enough to make her forget she was still confined to this room. She could have only dreamed of something like this.

"How big do you need it?" Vivienne raised one eyebrow quizzically.

Lilly pulled out the corners to a laptop monitor size. "Whoa! What operating system is it? How do I find the keyboard?" She turned the interface over examining all sides of it.

Vivienne sighed, taking the TAC from Lilly's hands. She sat it upright on the table.

"Good morning, Ida. Please display a dark web interface and a localized QWERTY keyboard."

"Good morning, Vivienne. In what language would you like the keyboard to be displayed?" the artificial interface replied and opened a Tor browser on the display.

Vivienne looked at Lilly for the answer. Lilly's mouth gaped open as she stared ahead. Vivienne smacked her lightly on the shoulder with the back of her hand, bringing her out of her trance.

"Oh, um, English."

A light display keyboard appeared on the table in front of the interface, beyond Lilly's comfortable reach. She took off her jacket and stretched her hands to an awkward position to type. She was astonished she could feel the keys above the table as solid as any mechanical keyboard.

Vivienne shook her head. This day was becoming more painful by the minute. She picked up the keyboard display, angling it up by twenty degrees, sliding it closer to Lilly.

"Better?"

"Thank you." Lilly hadn't felt this ridiculous in a very long time.

It didn't take long until she had found what she was looking for. Her contact's username was already inactive as she assumed it would be. She picked a few strings and ran a few rabbit holes until the trail had gone cold.

"That's the end of it. He's gone."

"For you maybe. Ida, track and trap. Notify security teams when the subject is located."

"Track and trap initiated. Is there anything else I can assist you with, Vivienne?" Ida asked.

"No thank you Ida. End interface."

The TAC pulled in the digital interfaces and folded itself back into a gum packet-sized bar of metal.

"Is that how you found me? A simple track and trap?" Lilly asked. She was disgusted by her hubris, thinking she couldn't be caught.

Vivienne laughed. "Don't be daft. You copied the file before you sent it. We tracked the file."

"Why can't you track the file to the buyer then?"

"Because you kept the original file. You sent the copy. Your equipment stripped the tracking program embedded in the file. You shouldn't have been able to do that."

Vivienne turned her attention away from Lilly. She had made a decision that was certain to be controversial.

"Oh. Sorry," Lilly apologized, watching Vivienne walk to the other side of the table.

Vivienne rubbed her head then leaned over the back of her chair, facing Lilly.

"Lilly, you're twice as good as any human at this, but you are so far behind the community. We want you to come home. No one is asking you to live in a clan. Just, come back to the community."

"Thanks for the offer, Vivienne, but I can't follow your rules. I'm not mate material. I'm not even clan material."

"No one is asking you to be. The community is in a transition, the laws are changing. Our whole system is changing. This time next year, we're not even going to be living on this planet. Most of us won't be, anyway. A few of the old guard are choosing to stay behind, afraid they can't adapt to the new ways." Vivienne studied Lilly's stunned expression.

It took Lilly a few seconds before she burst out laughing. "Bwahaha! Oh, hell! I can't breathe. Aah! You almost got me, Vivienne. Right up to the moving to another fucking planet part." Lilly stood up pacing and fanning herself. "I laughed so hard I almost peed myself. I'm supposed to believe we're all gonna go live on Mars in a sweet little vampire community? Who the hell are you? And what the fuck do you really want with me?"

"Have your laugh, Lilly. I get it. It's hard to swallow at first. I can't say I took the idea much better the first time I heard it."

"So, you're sticking with the whole 'moving to space' story. Super advances in technology, no blood necessary. You're fucking crazy, so I think I'll pass. How about you just open that door now and I can go home?"

Vivienne stood up raising her hands in surrender. "Absolutely, no problem. I told you before, we're not going to keep you against your will. Do you mind checking your phone for the time before we leave the building? I don't seem to have mine on me." Vivienne motioned toward Lilly's jacket hanging on the back of her chair. "Go ahead, it's still in your pocket."

Lilly took out her phone without breaking eye contact with Vivienne. She unlocked it with her fingerprint then looked down.

"It's 0830. You had me knocked out for almost an entire day? Where the hell are we?"

"No, look again. It's the same day." Vivienne pointed toward the phone.

"It's six hours earlier than when you abducted me. How is that possible? What did you do to my phone?" Lilly looked suspicious and confused.

"Check your location. You're not in Amsterdam, Lilly. You were only out for an hour."

"I'm not buying any of this. If we're in ..." she looked down, "*Montana*? I've had to have been out a lot longer than an hour." Lilly was in disbelief.

"Nope. Not possible with the time change. It's 1630 in Amsterdam right now. We're eight hours behind in Montana. We've been talking for an hour. You were out for an hour."

"I don't believe you, Vivienne. There is no way we could have gotten to Montana in an hour from Amsterdam."

"You were ported here," Vivienne stated calmly.

"Teleported? Open the fucking door, Vivienne." Lilly grabbed her jacket from the chair, stomping toward the door.

"Ida, open the door." Vivienne walked behind, letting Lilly lead the way. She'd never find the way out, but she was about to see some very confusing things.

The corridors were dimly lit. As the women walked down the hall, lights came up in front of them and dimmed behind them. She let Lilly walk ahead without speaking. Vivienne was relieved to see a familiar face heading toward them.

Lilly plastered her back against the wall, taking in the young man's scent as he approached. Her senses were betraying her. He didn't smell right. He wasn't human or vampire. He was tall, slender, and muscular at the same time. Short, black hair framed large, green eyes. Perfect skin, at least what she could see of it. He was dressed in black tac pants, a long-sleeved black T-shirt, and black boots. Military style. Lilly's mind raced. Fight or flee?

"Erik, dear, when you see Jack can you tell him he needs to discuss the cummerbund color with Violet. She's wavering between crimson and scarlet."

"Is that for the wedding or the turning?" Erik asked, ignoring Lilly attempting to melt into the wall beside him, her nostrils flaring.

"The turning, of course. The wedding cummerbund is white." Vivienne rolled her eyes as she grasped his hands.

He leaned down to kiss her on both cheeks. "Does it really matter? You've already picked the color for them, haven't you?"

"Don't be foolish. Of course, I have. He still needs to feel important. He is the groom after all, isn't he?"

"Well, I'm headed to the lab now. I'll let him know the second I get there." Erik began to walk away. Vivienne placed her hand on his arm prompting him to turn around.

"Ma'am?"

"Don't forget, I need you both back at the vineyard on Tuesday. The holographic screens are being installed in the new reception hall and I don't trust those contractors without supervision."

"We'll be there, Vivienne." Erik promised, alleviating her concern. He tapped behind his ear displaying a clock that only he could see. "I hope I'm not being rude, but I'm late." He turned, took three steps, and disappeared into a swirl of distorted air appearing in front of him. As the distortion closed, there was a noticeably light suctioning sound.

Vivienne turned back around to see Lilly staring into the space where Erik had disappeared, her mouth agape. Vivienne pushed Lilly's mouth closed with one finger.

"Careful dear, you don't want to attract flies." Vivienne smiled, wildly amused by Lilly's reaction.

"Wha … wha? What was that?" She stammered, shaking, as she extended her finger toward the spot Erik had disappeared from.

"The port? Just your standard spatial distortion that allows travel between places. I believe I already mentioned those."

Lilly was in a state of disbelief. "Uh. Uh-huh. And uh … and what was he?"

"Erik? He's Æsir. And maybe a little Vanir. We're not completely sure. He's one of Grace's triplets." Vivienne scrutinized her for signs of shock. It wouldn't be unusual.

"Grace? I thought nobody knew what she was or where she came from." Lilly was still speaking slowly and appeared dazed.

"No one did until about a year ago. I told you a lot has changed, Lilly. You're not going to pass out on me, are you? Because I'm not carrying you anywhere in these shoes." Vivienne placed a hand on her shoulder, prying her off the wall.

"Uh-huh." Lilly looked up at Vivienne, shaking her head 'no.'

"I think you need a drink," Vivienne smirked.

"Do, uh … do they have coffee here?"

Ida answered, interpreting the question as a request for directions. "Please follow the green lights on the floor to the dining facility located on this level."

Lilly jumped at the sound of Ida's voice coming from nowhere and everywhere at the same time.

"Thank you, Ida," Vivienne replied.

"My pleasure, Vivienne."

Vivienne and Lilly sat down at a high-top table in the far corner of the dining hall. Everything in the facility was sleek. Black and white, metal and glass, dotted with occasional pops of a bold accent color designating different sections or purposes. Color was sparingly used as a decorative element. An assortment of herbs and other plants in blue pots, sitting along an incredibly realistic faux window wall, was the extent of the nonessential color in this room.

A service unit approached to take their order. Lilly leaned toward the unit, sniffing at it, then breathing its scent.

Vivienne turned to the service unit. "My apologies for my friend, Betty," she said, reading the unit's nametag. "She's new. We'll take two coffees, please."

"Would you like anything else?" Betty asked, glancing at an ogling Lilly.

Vivienne looked at Lilly, who was too distracted to hear the question. "We'll discuss that after our coffee comes. Thank you, Betty."

Betty left to get their coffee.

"Was that AI? It smelled like electrically charged air," Lilly whispered.

"First of all, that was rude. She is a highly evolved, synthetic intelligence service unit. She is self-aware and is considered a silicate life form. I understand you're in a mild state of shock, but you need to be aware of your behavior. And her name is Betty if you hadn't noticed."

Lilly swallowed uncomfortably, flushing red with embarrassment. "You know, Viv, I'm close to a thousand years old. Until today, I thought I was the best of the best when it came to computers and cutting-edge tech. And today," she tapped her finger on the table, "right now I feel like a little girl playing at being an adult. It's like I'm a child sitting in a room filled with gods."

Vivienne couldn't even be upset with Lilly for calling her 'Viv'. She let it slide.

"You are. Not that I mean you're a child. I mean, you are sitting in a room with gods. Or, more correctly, life forms that some humans consider gods. For instance, directly behind me, on the far side of the room."

Lilly nodded.

"The man with the curly golden hair? We call him Leo. You may know him as Asclepius, God of medicine."

Lilly's eyes got wide as she pressed her back against the chair. She wasn't used to being surprised or shocked by anything.

"He's just a guy, Lilly. A really nice guy," Vivienne continued.

Betty approached with two cups of coffee and an assortment of plant-based sweeteners and creams.

"Thank you, Betty." Lilly smiled hesitantly.

"You're welcome. Did you decide on food?"

Vivienne answered, "No, I think coffee will be fine."

Betty nodded, leaving the women to their conversation.

"Keep looking at the same table. Kitty-corner from Leo. Longer, wavy dark hair, beard, dangerously gorgeous blue eyes. That's

Ben. Ben is Baldur. He's also just a guy. A very cranky, often rude, temperamental guy. From what I've heard, he wasn't always like that. Just since Asgard was destroyed, which would be reason enough for anyone to be a little angry. It's why the few remaining Æsir are here. Ben runs this facility, so he's under a tremendous amount of stress. You may want to avoid him, if possible," Vivienne nodded quickly. "Yes, I think I'd most definitely suggest that."

"And the others?" Lilly asked.

Vivienne casually scanned the room. "I don't recognize anyone else in here. I've only been here a few times myself. From what I hear, we also get a revolving carousel of others running through the place. Kali, Bevvi, Ma'at, Thoth, Tao, whoever. I suggest you learn to expect the unexpected if you plan on sticking around. It helps if you're not starstruck."

Lilly was beginning to regain her mental footing. "Did they bring us the blood substitute? What did you call it? CB?" She motioned with her head toward Ben and Leo.

Vivienne hadn't thought about it in that manner. "Yes and no. Our researchers had been looking for a blood substitute for about a hundred years. To keep testing consistent, they used Grace's blood. It was the perfect base. She was part of the community, and she was immortal but not vampire. Once they produced a clean blood product that worked, they no longer needed her as a source to produce the CB. All they needed was a pure sample of the dried base from which all CB is now produced. So, no, it was our scientists who produced it and, yes, it was from them because it was created from Grace's blood. And she is one of them."

"This is a lot to take in," she shook her head still unsure if this was real or a delusion induced by the drugs. Lilly scanned the room, letting her eyes land on a small group of humanoids. They were dressed differently than the others. The average person here wore black tac gear. Others, like Leo, dressed in silvery blue with what she considered a lab coat. The group at the table had a flexible style of armor. Lilly pinpointed her focus to see it was a tightly woven mesh probably made of carbon fiber or similar material. It had an overlay that appeared to be nearly colorless on top of the black undergarment. The group's skin color was diverse, ranging from light tan to a deep, rich brown, appearing more dimensional and thicker than the skin of a human. The main thing that made them stand out to Lilly, aside from their scent, was their eyes. No matter what their eye color, golden, lighted rings surrounded the corneas. They were most definitely warriors.

"Jur," Vivienne said. "And don't stare. They don't appreciate it much."

"What's their armor made of?" Lilly's curiosity was getting the best of her. Delusion or not, she was accepting the uniqueness of this new world as her curiosity was taking over. She wanted to know everything.

"I'm pretty sure the cloth is woven carbon fiber, and the armor layer is structured graphene of some sort. I'm not the best authority on high tech materials, so take what I said with a grain of salt. It sounds right in my head. That doesn't mean it's a practical application." Vivienne enjoyed practical implementation of technology. She preferred to leave the scientific aspects of it to the experts.

Lilly continued to take in the variety of beings gathered for breakfast as she sipped her coffee. Vivienne finished her cup and placed it on a pad in the center of the table, from which it disappeared. Lilly was more curious than startled, reaching out to examine the pad. It felt like regular glass, slick and cool to the touch.

"If you're finished, we need to get going. We have a few stops to make." Vivienne stood up.

"You ask me if I want to stay and now you want me to leave?" Lilly was perplexed.

"You're still bait for the time being, Lilly. And bait needs to be far away from the henhouse. Don't worry, you won't be bored where you're going." Vivienne smiled and started walking back toward the interrogation center monitoring room.

Lilly followed closely behind, taking two steps for each one of Vivienne's. She walked faster than expected for someone wearing four-inch pumps.

CHAPTER THREE

Vivienne burst through the door of the security control room, startling the guards. They were watching the monitors cycle through the different holding rooms. A black screen displayed the feed that should have been Lilly's interview room.

"Could you hand me my bag? We're leaving now." Vivienne addressed Jackass One with a sickly-sweet smile.

"You're taking the prisoner with you? That's not … I need to report this to Ivan." Jackass Two stood up.

Vivienne sighed with irritation. She shook her head. "You don't seem to have figured out the situation just yet, so I'll explain it to you. Lilly is working with us. She is our bait to catch the people who wanted the list. They won't find her if she's here, so I am taking her to where they will be able to find her. And you both owe her an apology. The restraints were over the top. You were supposed to pick her up quietly, not abduct her violently. Now I need to figure out a scenario detailing her plausible escape."

"We weren't given that information. We were only doing our jobs," Jackass Two defended.

"That didn't sound remotely like an apology." Vivienne shot him a look hard enough to pierce his skin.

Jackass One stepped forward and extended his hand with Vivienne's bag, while focusing his gaze on Lilly. "What he meant to say was, had we known, we wouldn't have treated you so roughly." Jackass One was less than enthusiastic about being cordial to Lilly.

Lilly was uncomfortable and embarrassed standing in the hall, as Vivienne snatched her bag away from the guard.

"Not quite the apology she's owed, but acceptable enough." Vivienne snapped around, letting the door slam behind her. She began walking quickly in the direction opposite from the one they came. She pulled out her TAC and began typing.

"Vivienne, why did you lie to them?" Lilly asked timidly.

Vivienne didn't slow her speed, nor look up from her TAC. "Are you working with us?"

"Yes, I guess so." Lilly struggled to keep up with her pace.

"Are you remorseful for your part in accessing the list?"

"Yes."

"Are you considering coming home? To the community?"

"Yes."

"Tell me, how would it have served anyone's best interest for your reputation to be marred by a single mistake that would have presumed you a traitor?" Vivienne turned into another corridor.

"I guess it wouldn't."

"The community needs people like you, Lilly. Out there is a vast universe of species, cultures, technologies, things we're only beginning to grasp. You have a mind that can embrace that kind of life. You will thrive out there. You will help all of us thrive out there."

"I can't say I wouldn't be happy about a fresh start."

Vivienne spun around holding her TAC out to one side and placed her free hand on her hip. She cocked her head to the right. "How many languages do you speak?"

Lilly breezed gracefully sideways to keep from mowing Vivienne down. "Twelve. Why?"

"So, English isn't the only one with rules regarding double negatives?" Indirect communication, in any language, was a pet peeve of Vivienne's.

Lilly narrowed her eyes into a mild scowl. "Has anyone ever told you you're a control freak?"

"Yes." Vivienne continued walking as fast as she had been prior to her sudden stop.

The corridor ended in a dimly lit open space with a row of cubicle style, opaque partitions lining its left side. Each cube was padded and contained a floating platform with a dark dome on the top. Some were open, and some were closed with people inside. Outside the cubicles were three-dimensional stat displays for monitoring their respective pods. Two technicians watched the displays.

The right side of the room had an elevator-sized platform next to the far wall, inset evenly with the floor.

"What is this place?" Lilly whispered.

"Why are you whispering?" Vivienne whispered back.

"Because it's dark and quiet," Lilly replied.

"It's a multi-purpose room. The pods are standard med pods which are being used as sleep pods." Vivienne waved her hand toward the cubicles. "They can't hear you. The hoods are noise canceling. We're not here for that. We're here for this." Vivienne turned to the pad behind them, pointing to the floor. "But not until I talk to one of them." She nodded behind her as she backed away from Lilly.

Lilly followed Vivienne across the room to one of the technicians.

"Ruzzio?" Lilly recognized him as he spun around to the sound of her voice. "You lazy piece of shit! They just let anybody in here, don't they?" she asked, staring him down.

"If it's not my favorite dysfunctional psychopath?" Ruzzio chuckled.

"I have empathy. Just not for you," Lilly replied cheekily, punching him in the arm.

"What are you doin' here?" He swept Lilly up in a headlock, although he was only about four inches taller than she was. Lilly tapped out and Ruzzio released his grip.

"I take it you two know each other." Vivienne didn't phrase it as a question, nor did she give them time to answer. "Ruzzio, I thought you'd be Italian."

"Mm, my dad was. My mother was Puerto Rican. I was blessed with romantic genes on both sides." Ruzzio extended his hand toward Vivienne. "And you are?"

"Vivienne … Eliassen." Vivienne peered at him smugly shaking his hand.

"My apologies ma'am. I just assumed since you were with Lilly … and … uh," Ruzzio was incredibly uncomfortable to learn he had just said something offensive in front of a Board member's mate. The way Vivienne looked at him made him feel even more uncomfortable.

"I don't care." Vivienne released his hand dismissively. "I need you to fit Lilly with some light body armor that will be undetectable under her clothing."

Ruzzio tugged on Lilly's sleeve. "By the looks of this outfit, you could hide a full suit of chainmail underneath there."

"We were hoping for something a little lighter," Vivienne smirked.

"Do I get an opinion?" Lilly asked.

"Certainly. Full plate medieval armor or something lighter?" Vivienne mocked.

Lilly rolled her eyes. "Just make it black."

"No problem. Half an hour. You want to use a sleep pod while I'm gone?" Ruzzio offered Vivienne.

"Yes, thank you." Vivienne wouldn't pass on this opportunity. She'd love to have one of these for the vineyard.

"Ten is open." Ruzzio nodded toward the cube and Vivienne was off.

"You want to try it, Lilly? It's the best sleep you'll ever have. Six hours in twenty minutes."

"Sure. What do I do?"

Ruzzio waved the other technician over. "Harmon will take care of you." Ruzzio slapped Harmon on the back, turned and ported out.

Lilly was sure she would eventually get used to seeing that. Today had been rough. As far as her body was concerned, she had only been up for about twelve hours. Her brain felt like it had been days. She followed Harmon to an open pod. The floating platform was set too high for her to climb up. Harmon smirked, but not in a mean way. He reached forward, touching the corner. A small digital interface lit under the surface that allowed him to lower it for her.

"It'll be more comfortable if you take your jacket off. You can hang it on the wall."

Lilly didn't see a hook as she took her jacket off. She looked between the wall and Harmon. Harmon took the jacket from her and, as he placed it against the wall, a hook slid out, catching the jacket. Lilly climbed up onto the platform. There was so much to get used to. She hoped this nap didn't turn out to be something permanent.

She laid down expecting the comfort of a hard examination table, but found it felt like being swaddled in a warm cloud. Harmon pulled the hood down to cover her torso. It was warm, dark, and quiet. She could make out the slightest hint of white noise before dropping off.

Feeling as if only seconds had passed, she opened her eyes to find Vivienne standing over her.

"How did you like it?"

Usually feeling groggy when she woke, fifty years ago, it would have taken a pot of coffee and half a pack of smokes before she felt normal. These days, two cups gave Lilly the jump-start she needed to begin her day, and she hadn't touched nicotine in decades. Not this time. It was an odd feeling to be wide awake and focused before she had even sat upright. She wasn't only clear, she was crisp. Clean was the best way for her to describe it. Mentally clean. All the cloudiness had been lifted. Her senses were sharp.

"Not sure yet. I feel different." Lilly sat up, dangling her feet off the side.

"These things really clean out the cobwebs, don't they?" Vivienne handed Lilly her jacket.

"That's one way to put it." Lilly hopped off the platform and slipped her jacket on, only it wasn't her jacket. It looked like hers, but the material was different. She patted herself down, feeling the pockets. Everything was there, all her stuff in all the right places.

"Everything is there." Vivienne saw her searching for something.

"It isn't my jacket."

"Ruzzio thought it would be better to give you something people were used to seeing you wear. He also left you a couple of impact absorbing T-shirts." Vivienne handed Lilly a cloth bag with an assortment of black, gray, and white long and short sleeved T-shirts.

"I don't understand the necessity. Bullets won't kill us."

"No, but they do slow us down. You can avoid a bullet if you know it's coming. Unaware, or caught from multiple angles, you could take several rounds. All of them would disable you for a time. These shirts will also keep a dart from piercing your skin."

"And that's how you got me, isn't it?" Lilly asked, glad to be firing on all cylinders again.

"Yes," Vivienne said flatly.

Lilly took the bag out of Vivienne's hand.

"Are you ready?" Vivienne asked as she began walking away.

"Wait. Where are we going?"

Vivienne turned back to face Lilly. "First, we are going to my family's vineyard in Canada, so I can change. I didn't expect to be playing escort today. Second, we are going to the shit hole you refer to as an apartment to collect your things. And then we are taking you to my brother's vineyard in Italy, where we have an advantage over anyone coming for you."

"Or I can disappear on my own."

"Which would defeat the entire purpose of letting you know you are bait," Vivienne said coldly, raising her eyebrow.

"I thought you didn't decide to make me bait until after you caught me," Lilly snapped back.

"No. We were always planning to make the hacker bait. I decided to let you in on the plan once they told me you were one of us. I told you from the very start, I was your way out. If you hadn't been a vampire, you were going to be tagged and returned right back to where we got you. We would have monitored you, hopefully preventing you from getting yourself killed."

"Meaning, if I disappear now, it defeats your whole plan to catch this person or people?"

"No, wrong again, Lilly. It means you will be on your own. It defeats my plan to keep you alive, it doesn't mean we can't monitor you." Vivienne thought this woman was supposed to be smart. She might be technically savvy, but she certainly wasn't sly or cunning as everyone thought she was.

"Ah, my venom. You can locate me through my venom, can't you?" Lilly deduced. The unexpected nature of the day still had her on her back foot. She was catching up.

"Yes. Are you ready to go now?" Vivienne turned, resuming her direction and pace.

Lilly followed looking at several people who had also finished with their pod time. She spied a familiar face.

"Vivienne isn't that the man you met in the hallway. Erik?"

"No." Vivienne didn't even look. She could tell by his energy and his scent. "That's Alex."

"You didn't say they were identical triplets. How do you tell them apart?"

"Aside from scent, their vibrations are different. Erik is much calmer, rational. Mikkel is very high energy and scattered. Alex is outwardly arrogant, abrasive and inwardly more sensitive than the other two." Vivienne hesitated at the edge of the platform on the other side of the room, waiting for Lilly to catch up.

She stepped on the platform and waved her hand over the side wall. As the screen lit up, she entered a code and pointed to a spot beside her where Lilly needed to stand. "Come on."

"Come on where?" Lilly stepped forward.

As soon as Lilly's back foot had broken the imaginary line of the platform boundary, Vivienne tapped the green light on the panel. Lilly's world swirled in front of her, sending her out of balance. She caught Vivienne's sleeve and swore she could see a hint of a smile on her face. The motion lasted only a fraction of a second. Lilly was facing a chiseled stone wall. She ran her fingers over a cold, rough surface. It was white, pink, and light gray with sparkling flecks.

"Quartzite. This whole level is dug out of bedrock. Perfect for wine. Keeps the temperature and humidity constant," Vivienne explained. "This way." She stepped off an identical platform to the one they had previously been on.

Lilly had been facing the back of the port. She turned to see a cavernous space lined on the sides with racks of wine, stacked floor to ceiling. Additional rows jutted out eight feet perpendicular from the walls, spaced every four feet. A wide walkway ran down the length of the room ending at sealed glass doors. The lighting was dim, but past the doors, the light was bright, glistening off the walls. They turned right, moving past several corridors and a few private tasting rooms. She imagined it would be easy to get lost down here.

At the end of the hall stood an elevator large enough to fit a small forklift. Everything here appeared shiny and new. When the doors opened on the upper floor, it wasn't what Lilly would have imagined. The main event hall was a phenomenal space, rivaling some of the small museums she had seen. Smooth marble walls and floors ran throughout, edged by columns carved with intricately detailed grape vines. The views out the tall windows matched some of the best anywhere in her memory. The wall behind her was fully covered with a muted fresco. Tasteful artwork and carvings adorned every surface that wasn't glass. All this beauty held in by a two and a half story vaulted roof. Lilly liked the feel of the enormous space - old and modern at the same time. A perfect blend that could be dressed for any occasion.

Construction had been recently finished, judging by the stack of leftover materials outside. Lilly could also see a construction dumpster in an area she thought likely to be outdoor seating when it was finished.

"So, this is how the other side lives," Lilly said more to the air than to Vivienne, as she soaked in the grandeur of the main room.

"It'll add to the resale value." Vivienne's statement was somber.

"Why would you sell? Didn't you just build it?" Lilly asked with bewilderment.

"It'll be sold to fund the community members choosing to stay behind. We won't be living here by the end of next year." As excited as Vivienne was about moving to the new colony on Rasa, she was saddened to leave this place. She had poured her heart into making it exactly what she wanted. She had hoped to have it in the family for centuries to come.

"You have got to have at least one huge bash in this place before that. Kind of a final send-off. It'd be a waste not to." Lilly craned her neck, taking in the details of the ceiling.

"Don't worry about that. The wedding we have planned for this place will be the event of the century." Vivienne displayed a muted excitement that contrasted with her normally stoic refinement.

"Wedding? Those are nothing more than a huge waste of money. The bride and groom are miserable, never getting what they really want while being forced to be gracious to hordes of people they barely know or like." Lilly turned to see Vivienne glaring at her. "What? They are," Lilly defended.

"We don't judge what may or may not make others happy, Lilly."

Vivienne's hard, plastic smile made Lilly slightly afraid in the way a child is scared of a plastic clown. It was an unusual feeling for Lilly. Not much scared her these days. *Who is this woman?* she thought, turning away awkwardly to examine one of the art pieces nearby.

"I," Vivienne raised an eyebrow at Lilly, "am going down to the house to change. You can wait here. The building is interfaced with Ida. You may ask her for anything you need while I'm gone." Vivienne had disappeared before Lilly turned back around.

Lilly wandered the upper floor, making her way to the kitchen at the back. She requested a hot chocolate from Ida. It was amazing - a rich, dark chocolate blended with the perfect amount of sugar and cream. Hints of vanilla bean, cinnamon and chili finished it off. Cup in hand, she walked out onto the side deck. It was cold with a light biting breeze. She pulled up her hood. Her jacket was keeping her comfortable, although it shouldn't have been. It was too light. At least her old jacket would have been too light. This new one was perfect. Not too hot to wear when she was indoors, yet it kept her warm in temperatures well below what it should have. The material had to be thermal regulating. It was the only reasonable explanation she could think of.

She leaned on the wide railing. The view of the mountain was peaceful, covered in white. A blanket of snow cascaded down dotted by trees and the occasional jutting rock until finally being broken by a stream of water, flowing under the surface of the frozen pond. It was late afternoon. This time of year, the valley was already beginning to take on the mountain's shadow, casting a bluish tint onto the blanket of fresh snow. It would be getting dark soon.

Lilly heard footsteps behind her. Two sets. She turned to see Vivienne dressed in a pair of tight jeans and black wellies, a pink and black flannel shirt covered with a thick pink cable knit sweater and a down jacket. The outfit was topped off with a black hat and gloves. If Lilly hadn't been familiar with her scent, she would have thought her an entirely different person. She was followed closely by another woman about an inch taller with long deep auburn red hair, dressed in a green, similar fashion.

"Lilly, this is my daughter, Violet."

Lilly's mind flashed back to the hallway. Erik, Violet, Jack, cummerbund, groom … shit. She wasn't about to apologize for having her own opinion. She might have thought about sharing it had she known it was Vivienne's daughter getting married.

"Nice to meet you." Lilly extended her hand to Violet.

Violet shook it with a firm grip. "Likewise."

"Excuse me. I have a few things to take care of before we leave." Vivienne didn't wait for a reply. She was already back inside.

"This ridiculously huge wedding is nine months away and she acts like it's nine days away. I'll be so glad when it's over." Violet leaned against the rail next to where Lilly had been.

Lilly didn't feel nearly as bad for saying what she had after Violet's statement. "Why does it need to be so big? I mean, if you don't want a big wedding, why don't you elope or something?"

"You did spend most of the day with my mother, didn't you?"

"Yeah. She is kind of … how should I put it? Driven." Lilly shrugged, hoping she hadn't offended Violet.

"Sure. We'll go with that," Violet giggled.

"She seems pretty tough."

"She can be. She's empathetic, too. She just doesn't let people see it. I'll deny I said it if you tell her, but she likes you, Lilly," Violet said.

Lilly snorted.

"You wouldn't be here if she didn't. She would have left you in that cell. She definitely would not have brought you to our home."

"I haven't actually seen your home," Lilly raised an eyebrow.

"Semantics. You're on the property." Violet waved her hand. "She wouldn't be doing any of this for you if she didn't like you."

"She has a strange way of showing it."

"Don't let her hard-exterior fool you. She had a difficult life. She has a soft spot for outcasts and orphans."

"I figured she'd never had anything worse than a broken fingernail. Wasn't she born a vampire?"

"No, she was human. My father found her a few hours after she was beaten, gutted, and left for dead in an alley. He turned her without the Board's permission. While they were on probation, she went over the top in the perfect appearance direction. It's kind of stuck."

"That's something we have in common. Not the perfect appearance part, as you can see. But the left for dead part. My sire found me unconscious. Whoever they were, rescued me, turned me, and left me before I woke up. She was left for dead. I was left for undead," Lilly chuckled.

"I told you she was partial to orphans," Violet laughed with her.

Vivienne walked back out behind them. "Everyone ready?"

Lilly questioned Violet, "Are you coming with us?"

"Your apartment doesn't have a port platform. Mother hasn't much personal porting experience, but I do it all the time. I live in Napa, but the wedding is here, so, you know. I port, a lot." Violet rolled her eyes and exaggerated a tongue out expression of exhaustion while facing Lilly, with her mother behind her.

Lilly looked down and snickered at Violet, trying to hide her amusement from Vivienne.

"Ready," Violet said, as she pirouetted toward her mother.

Lilly downed the remaining few drops of her hot chocolate. She was nervous. Porting from a platform that was designed for that specific activity was difficult enough to wrap her head around. How was she supposed to grasp the concept that ordinary vampires, like her, had the ability to port? She mustered up her last bit of courage and set the cup on the rail. "Ready."

Violet gave Lilly a reassuring smile. "Lilly, you're the navigator, so you're in the middle."

"Navigator?" Lilly questioned.

"You know our destination, so you're the navigator. It's simple. Get a clear picture of our destination, preferably a clear space where we won't land on anything." Violet watched Lilly's expression. No signs of panic.

Lilly felt a rush of heat over her body. She tried to look calm, but she was sure they could hear her heart pounding. She swallowed hard, grasping the other two women's hands. "Okay. Oh, shit. Wait!" Lilly broke the connection and ran inside.

Vivienne and Violet exchanged confused glances. Lilly hadn't seemed to be the kind that would bolt. And it wasn't like she had anywhere she could go.

Lilly came back out, holding up the cloth bag Ruzzio had given Vivienne. "I almost forgot these." She slipped the handle over her wrist, regaining her position between Violet and Vivienne. "Okay, now I'm ready."

She thought about her apartment in Amsterdam, and they stepped through the port Violet opened.

CHAPTER FOUR

It wasn't an apartment as much as it was a converted warehouse. They walked to the center of the open space. Vivienne's eyes roamed over everything, shocked at the simplicity. It was nothing like what she was expecting. Lilly had the top floor of the building converted into an industrial loft. The upper space, a quarter the size of the lower living area, was an open sleeping nook. The long sides were flanked with floor to ceiling windows of black, industrial metal-lined, meter-square grids of thermal, double paned glass. The commercial style kitchen lay directly beneath the sleeping loft and the end walls were concrete with metal and glass light fixtures. Exposed ductwork and metal conduit piping painted black, completed the base style allowing the finishes and fixtures to stand out. The overall look appeared very high end.

A large shelving unit against the wall opposite the kitchen was filled with completed canvases. Leaning against the concrete pillars were more paintings and line drawings. Close to one side of the room was an easel beside a table overflowing with paints, buckets, pencils, brushes, chalk, rags, and mixing boards. Against the table were stacked both stretched and unstretched canvases in several different sizes. The art itself was an eclectic mix: portraits, expressionist, watercolors, landscapes, and some very intricate modern line art. Closer to Lilly's computer setup was a wide format printer skirted by several pieces of digital art. Another large shelving unit behind the desk held books that, by the looks of them, housed some that were hundreds of years old. Lilly had an exceptional eye for detail. It wasn't only her talent that surprised Vivienne, but also her range. Most surprising was seeing Lilly express a full color pallet.

Lilly smirked. "Not the shit hole you were expecting?"

"No. You have more depth than I had credited you with." Vivienne scanned the room again. She wasn't often so wrong about someone and didn't have a problem admitting it. "You did all of these?" She stretched her hands out motioning to the canvasses.

"I did," Lilly answered simply.

"May I?" Violet asked, placing her hand on a large sketch book in one of the art cubes.

"Have at it. I'm sure when whoever wanted the list comes after me and finds this place, they'll burn it to the ground." Lilly didn't much care.

There were only a few things she wanted to take with her. She picked up an art portfolio, a laptop, and a few canvases, stacking them in the middle of the room. She headed upstairs to grab some of her clothes. She already had a go bag packed with her most important assets. She stuffed a few more things into the bag. Living the lifestyle she did, she never knew when she would be traveling or would need to bolt forever. She had lived in this place for close to fifty years, yet she wasn't sad to leave it. She had done all the construction work on the space herself. The expensive looking finishes were inexpensive materials and salvage pieces when she originally installed them. The black, white, and gray surfaces were created to be background for her art. She was happy with the way it had turned out. She was also excited to be leaving. In all the time she had lived, she seldom thought there would be anything different aside from the art she created or the technology she loved. Lilly easily closed chapters in her life when it was time for a new adventure. And she had a feeling this adventure would be epic.

"I'm ready," Lilly said, as she scanned what she was leaving behind.

Vivienne also scanned the room. "What about your art? You're going to leave all this behind?"

"It's served its purpose," Lilly replied.

"It seems a shame to let all of it go. Are you sure?" Violet looked sadly at the pages of a sketchbook.

Lilly smiled wistfully. "I have my memories. If you see something you like, take it. I don't mind."

"What about these? Your designs are beautiful. This dress is incredibly elegant." Violet ran her fingers across the page. She could feel the pencil marks of the gold and silver brocade skirt dripping in crystals, under a silver metal corset. It wasn't just something special. It was stunning. She flipped through the pages, landing on a long, white, flowing gown with a draped neckline and multiple straps across the back forming an intricate pattern.

"May I have these?" Violet looked up biting her lower lip.

"Sure. All yours." Lilly would never have imagined someone would be interested in her designs. She had only doodled them to pass time.

"Thank you!" Violet jumped up, startling Lilly with a hug that she was less than eager to return.

"Ooookaaay. You can let go now." Lilly pried Violet's arms off her as she stepped back.

Lilly knelt down, stuffed her laptop inside her bag, draped it over her shoulder and picked up her portfolio. She then slipped two canvasses under her free arm.

"Do you mind grabbing those other two paintings?" she asked the women.

Violet picked them up, placing them gently under her arm and gripped the sketchbook tightly in her hand.

Vivienne spotted a few pieces she liked, making a mental note to come back for them. She wished she could save them all. It was a shame to let such beautiful work be abandoned.

Vivienne stepped between the two women, placing a hand on each of their shoulders. "My turn to navigate. Ready, Violet?"

Violet responded by opening a portal.

As they stepped out of the portal, they found themselves inside a courtyard, surrounded by a building of clay stucco, aged in hues of yellows and pinks, creating an overall look of amber. The courtyard faced a heavy wooden door with dense iron hinges and hardware. Curving at the top, the door fit perfectly into the opening. A large, rough looking man stepped out onto the flat stone. His black hair was short and unruly, his skin tan. He stepped toward them as Lilly caught his scent. He was one of them. Vivienne stepped forward, giving this giant a hug, and kissing him on both cheeks. They greeted each other in a familiar language that took a few seconds for Lilly to dissect as Italian. She hadn't heard that dialect in over a century, and her skills in speaking it were as rough as the man in front of her. She hoped he spoke English or French. Even Spanish would be easier to understand.

Vivienne pulled the man toward them as Violet greeted him next. Fortunately for Lilly, they spoke English to one another.

"Vito, this is Lilly. Lilly, this is my brother Vito," Vivienne introduced.

Lilly felt a wash of relief come over her as she extended her hand toward the man. "Thank you for inviting me into your home," she said, hesitantly. She wasn't sure what else she should say.

Vito ignored her extended hand placing his large, meaty hands on her shoulders. He bent down awkwardly and kissed her on both cheeks. "Please, come in. You are welcome to stay as long as you need."

He released her, pressing his hand into her back and leading her forward into the house. "Viv tells me you've gotten yourself into some trouble."

"I'm sorry to bring it to your home. I can leave if you don't want me here." The last thing Lilly wanted was someone else involved in her mess.

Vito scoffed loudly. "Don't be stupid girl. There's no better place for you to be. We take care of our own. You will stay."

Vito's accent was thick, but Lilly had no trouble understanding him. Vivienne and Violet followed them as he pushed Lilly through the door. The hallway was far more modern than the exterior had led her to believe it would be. Everything was traditional, old-world style, but the materials were new. It had all the trappings of a modern villa. She was a little thrown off by how welcoming he was. She didn't get much of that from strangers.

"Alonzo!" Vito called out loudly.

A young man trotted down the hall toward them. He was somewhat attractive, much shorter than Vito, standing at about Violet's height. He was of mixed-race with light brown, curly hair and light, golden brown eyes, more of a hazel when he came close. He was also one of them.

"Bene, bene. We've been waiting for you. Good to see you make it inna one part." Alonzo's English was a little harder to understand than Vito's. Lilly would need to brush up on her Italian if she was going to be here long.

"Nice to meet you, Alonzo." Lilly extended her hand.

Alonzo stopped, uncertain what to make of the formal greeting before taking her hand in both of his and shaking it vigorously.

"Is that all of you to bring?" Alonzo pointed at her meager possessions.

Lilly flushed with embarrassment. "Yes, it's all that was important."

"Bene," Alonzo repeated.

"Alonzo, take Lilly's things up to Lukkas' room," Vito ordered.

"Oh, no. I don't want to put anyone out," Lilly said pleadingly.

"No trouble. Lukkas is in Canada. He won't be coming back here before going up into the sky with the others," Vito waved his hand as if he were shooing away a fly. He was an animated speaker. "Come, we eat, and we talk."

Alonzo was gathering Lilly's belongings as Vito ushered the women into the dining room. When they entered, there were five other vampires setting the long table and bringing in food. Of the two men helping, one was Hispanic and the other white. Two of the three women were mixed race, like Alonzo and the third was probably African tribal by her skin tone and jewelry. They were dressed much in the same way Vito was, wearing khaki field pants, white denim shirts and tan boots; casual and wrinkled, but not dirty.

Vivienne introduced them. They had all chosen to stay behind for their own reasons. Clans were settling and re-forming into smaller clans in places like this where they could live unnoticed … for a while anyway. When they sat down at the table, Alonzo came trotting in as he had before in the hallway. He took the empty seat beside Lilly. Vito was at the head of the table and Vivienne at the foot.

They all had a rudimentary grasp of English. A few spoke French, which Lilly was comfortable with. She hadn't expected any of them to speak Mandarin or any of the other eastern languages she was fluent in. They discussed light topics at first, like where did you come from, how old are you, and other topics of interest. And they were all astounded to discover Lilly was the oldest person at the table. In their world, looks were deceiving.

The food was exquisite, showcasing many pasta dishes, vegetables and something resembling seafood. There wasn't any real meat, which Lilly found unusual. A few of the dishes contained meat substitutes, which they grew in labs now. If they hadn't told her, she would never have known. She found the idea of vegetarian vampires hilarious. They still included cheese and eggs in their diet, but since their blood cravings had been satiated with CB, clean blood substitute, the community abstained from killing anything.

After they finished eating, close to two hours later, Vito addressed Lilly. "So, what do you know about the people coming after you?"

Before she could answer, Vivienne intervened. "All we know at this point is that they took the bait list. The facility is monitoring the people on the list to see whom they come after first. Lilly will be checking the chat room. Once they realize the list was not what they had expected it to be, she will need to lure them here. Ivan has arranged for sentinels to be staged on properties around the villa and in the two closest towns. Before Violet and I leave, we will reprogram the port with new security codes, which will only allow access from the facility and the vineyard at home in Canada. The rest is going to be a waiting game."

"Okay. So, we run the winery here as normal. Not that there's much to do until spring when the remaining families come here," Vito answered sternly.

Vivienne sighed. "I hope it doesn't take that long. Some of the older members of the community won't be as welcoming to Lilly as you are."

Lilly hung her head for a moment. She looked up at Vito. "If it does take that long, and they don't want me here when the elders come, I'll leave. I know what some others think of me for deserting the community after the exterminations. I don't blame them. But when many of them wanted revenge, I didn't want anything to do with it. After tempers had settled and Ivan had discouraged revenge on humans, it was too late for me to come back."

Violet placed her hand on Lilly's squeezing it gently. "It's never too late to come home, Lilly. At least not for those of us who have found a new one."

Lilly nodded and stared at her plate. She couldn't imagine a world where people lived in harmony, all wanting the best for each other, the way she saw the group at the facility in Montana doing. She had a hard time accepting a utopian existence could be real. She had a harder time accepting they would really want her to be a part of it. The two guards who abducted her didn't seem to want her included.

Violet released Lilly's hand. "Come on. Let's let mother and Vito work out the dull stuff while Alonzo and I give you the penny tour."

Alonzo got up quickly. "No, no, no. It cost no money. I give you for free."

Alonzo's eager grin was huge, lighting up his entire face. He grasped the back of Lilly's chair and slid it out so she could get up in a graceful manner. He then did the same for Violet. "Come."

The trio made their way back outside. It was cold and dry. There wasn't any snow as there had been at the other vineyard, although it was significantly windier here. They hiked to the top of one of the softly rolling hills. The landscape was brittle, crunching under her feet with each step. Winter views extended over gentle slopes onto the edges of the property. Lilly could see the shadows of dormant forests that would be lush with foliage come spring. There were a few small houses and cabins dotting the perimeter as far as she could see. Some people emerged from the structures to watch them momentarily before returning to the warm internal confines of the buildings. She was certain they were the security Vivienne had spoken about. If they hadn't been vampires, they wouldn't have been able to see them standing on the hill, from those distances, without binoculars. Oddly enough, it made her feel more comfortable. It was strange how having that many vampires so close together would make her feel that way. It normally would have unsettled her.

Alonzo pointed out the boundaries of the land they owned. The homes she saw would be occupied by community members joining the clan to work the land come spring, after they had wrapped up their affairs wherever they came from. The smaller numbers remaining here, on this small dot in the vastness of the universe, would need to group together to survive. How different things were going to be once the majority of the community left for a new world. Lilly was pulled out of her musing trance by Violet tugging on her sleeve.

"The wine cellars?" Violet repeated.

"Oh, yes. Sorry. You caught me daydreaming," Lilly giggled. She couldn't think of the last time she giggled. She so desperately wanted to trust these people, and at the same time, she didn't want that desperation to make her blind.

It was nearly dark when they got back to the villa. Everyone was lounging in the large room connected to the kitchen. The attached fireplace was a small room of its own. There was a large trough in the center with a blazing fire, and stone benches lined the walls. Lilly didn't have to duck to walk under the mantle. It took her back to the long forgotten keeping rooms all the largest houses used to have. As they entered, someone pushed a glass of wine into her hand. Wine wasn't her alcohol of choice, but she found this one soft, smooth and pleasing against her pallet. It was one that contained CB. It was funny to think, the more she drank, the more it quenched her thirst.

After Violet and Vivienne left, Alonzo showed her to her room, which was actually a suite of rooms. She had a small, private sitting area with a bank of windows on one side, and a built-in lounge underneath. On the other side was a large bookcase full of new reading material. It would be an excellent room for reading and painting. The bedroom itself wasn't huge, but it was large enough to hold a king-size bed. There were two closets to the side and a large, flat screen TV mounted on the wall opposite the bed. She could link her laptop to that, using it as a huge monitor if she wanted to do some digital renderings. *Sweet!* she thought. The last room that accompanied her suite was the bathroom. Again, it was a decent size but not huge. Big enough for two people if needed, with all the basic necessities and nice marble finishes.

Once Alonzo left her, she pulled out her laptop to see if there was any activity on the dead user account. There wasn't, so she decided to read. She perused the bookcase running her fingers along the spines before spotting a large blue book. It was so worn she couldn't read the title anymore, so she pulled it out. Inside of the cover, on the prologue page showed the words 'Here bygynneth the Book of the Tales of Caunterbury.' Lilly recognized it but had never had the opportunity to see one in the original old English. She didn't think it was a fourteenth century original, although it was several hundred years old. The pages smelled musty and the ink acidic, perfect for the cold, bitter evening.

She went downstairs for a cup of tea and was followed back to her room by a tiny chocolate and cream ball of fluff. He jumped into the chair Lilly was planning to read in, so she moved him to the floor and sat down. He stared at her as she picked up her book and started reading. She glanced down at him around the side of her book and sighed.

"Come on then," she said patting the cushion.

He jumped into her lap licking her face.

"Okay, that's enough," she laughed stroking his soft coat.

Lilly felt a tag against her thumb and pulled it out. "Grizz, huh? What a strange name for such an adorable little sweetie."

She gave him one final rub under the chin before he snuggled himself between her leg and the side of the chair. She guessed she had earned herself a reading partner.

CHAPTER FIVE

Two months had passed without the slightest sign of any investigation into the list. Who knew, maybe they hadn't been able to decode the encryption yet. For Lilly it wasn't difficult. Once she got to the vineyard, she hacked the buyer's upload site and downloaded a second copy, making sure to leave the tiniest of clues behind. By day three, without any of her normal tools, she had decrypted it. It shouldn't have taken even the most inept hacker longer than two weeks to decrypt. If anyone had the half dozen living serial killers and numerous other scum under surveillance, they sure were taking their sweet time doing anything with them. Who knows how many more innocent humans had died during that stretch. She was disgusted by the thought of humans taking other human lives for pleasure.

While she hadn't been explicitly placed on lockdown, Vito didn't like her wandering the property alone. Not that he thought Lilly was incapable of handling herself, but merely found it more reasonable to maintain a buddy system. If they lost Lilly, they lost their link to the buyer. It was more difficult to abduct someone if they weren't alone. That was something Lilly understood firsthand. She hadn't so much as smelled Vivienne's team when they took her.

She continued to busy herself indoors with reading, painting, and working on her Italian with Alonzo. She was trying hard to comply with what Vivienne had asked her to do. If it weren't so frustrating sitting around as bait, it would have been a peaceful vacation. Violet had visited a few times, informing Lilly she wanted to use the dress designs for her wedding. Lilly found it ironic being so vehemently against mating and marriage that her dresses would be the dream gowns for Violet's ceremony. Seeing how happy the designs made Violet, Lilly gave her blessing as long as Violet didn't expect her to attend.

Aside from the sporadic visits, there wasn't much to do on a vineyard in winter. So much for Vivienne's statement that she wouldn't be bored where she was going. There were things she could do, but she was used to going wherever she wanted, whenever she wanted. She hated feeling caged, reporting her whereabouts anytime she stepped outside to breathe. Lilly was possibly the oldest person left on the entire continent, and she felt like she was being treated like a naive child. The waiting game was the one game she despised.

Lilly was painting when Vivienne showed up again. This time with news one of the killers from the list had disappeared. The one who took children's fingers as mementos. Lilly had been using the TAC she received from the facility to monitor Ida's list tracking and wasn't surprised by Vivienne's visit three days after the news had come. Lilly was outwardly happy to have seen the news alert. Vivienne didn't admonish her for being glad it was that particular human that was taken. It was obvious these people were the scourge of the earth, or they wouldn't have been placed on that list.

Vivienne didn't appear as excited about it. "It wasn't that he was taken. It was the way he was taken. He walked into a rest stop bathroom and never came out. There were no other exits. His vehicle is still there. If I had to guess, I would say he was ported out. The only real gratifying news is that after the authorities found his vehicle, they also found his killing nest. There were two children still alive. They'll likely suffer with mental health issues for the remainder of their lives, but at least they'll have a chance. They also found evidence of more than thirty victims. As unfortunate as that is, at least it will provide some sense of closure for the families. And he's on their radar now, so if he ever shows up again, there's a probable chance he will be caught."

Vivienne sat in the lounge as she spoke, watching Lilly paint the view from her window. Her color sense was perfect. Vivienne was watching a master work her craft. The sky was crisp, incorporating several shades of blue and green. The grays and whites of wispy clouds and the subtle deep colors of dormant vines flowed from her brush. Everything was captured as clean as a photograph, including the window frame and the depth of the glass in front of her.

"So, we're right back where we were two months ago. No one saw anything. They didn't leave a trace," Lilly sighed putting down her brush.

"Hopefully, it won't take long for them to realize he's not a vampire when the wounds they inflict don't heal. If one of the others is taken soon, we will know. Just keep a closer eye out for any communication. At least it's something."

"I've set up an alert on my computer. If there's any contact, it will come through to my watch. Anything happens, I'll know within seconds." Lilly held up her arm showing the smart watch on her wrist. "When I back hacked the file, I left a tiny fragment of broken code revealing enough of an IP address to trace back to this area."

"I have no idea what that means. Can you link that alert to my phone?" Vivienne asked, holding hers out to Lilly.

"Sure." Lilly reached out to take it.

Vivienne unlocked it and handed it over. Lilly took a couple of swipes at it, entered a few strings of text linking it to her account, then handed it back.

"That's it?"

"Yup."

"Okay. Don't do anything until I get here." Vivienne stood up to leave.

"I wouldn't want them to think I was waiting for it. I figured I'd make them wait at least a few hours." Lilly shrugged. "It only makes sense."

"Yeah, cause all this makes sense." Vivienne said as she exited the room leaving Lilly to finish her painting.

It was another week of tedium for Lilly. She detested waiting, finding solace only in making art and reading new books. Her music was restricted to headphones, as Vito had made it clear he was unappreciative of her fondness for high volume and obscure new genres. He leaned toward the classical and operatic side of the spectrum, nearly always in Italian. Lilly didn't mind his musical taste, although hers bent more toward pieces with heavier bass and fewer woodwinds.

The simplicity of being in the country significantly contrasted with her usual chaotic existence. She had gotten used to the anonymousness of melting into dark backgrounds in urban landscapes. People didn't tend to notice girls like her in the busy streets. If they did notice, they avoided her. She resembled that of so many young runaways, coupled with the sharpness and skill of experience. Her speed allowed her to remove herself from view before she could be singled out. In crowded places, she was a ghost. Here, she was one of less than a dozen with skills closely matching hers.

While the others mostly left her alone, Alonzo seemed to think her youthful appearance indicated they had things in common. The exact opposite was closer to the truth. To Lilly, Alonzo was still an infant. He was a pure born vampire less than a quarter century old. His incessant questions gave her a headache. There was only so much time she could spend with him until she was ready to throttle him. He was hyper and excited by the minutest things. Lilly preferred a calmer companion; someone intellectual, whose voice didn't shatter her thoughts every ten seconds; someone she could sit in quiet comfort with. Alonzo was not that person.

He was a nice kid, and Lilly didn't want to shatter his enthusiasm for life. She also could not tolerate his annoyance on a consistent basis. The use of headphones turned into a blessing. Even when she could hear him, she was able to pretend she couldn't without offending him. It was unusual she cared about offending people. But then again, those were humans that she wasn't likely to encounter more than once. She was beginning to view these people as her people. Who knew how long she would be stuck here with them? And there was a fair chance that she would see at least one of them in the future. If she wanted a fresh start, she might as well start here by not belittling her hosts.

The TAC vibrated in her pocket, pulling her attention away from the book she was reading. She popped it up. Another scumbag taken off the street. This time it was a middle-aged woman who traded in babies. She would find high-risk girls - usually runaways or addicts - whore them out until they got pregnant, then take their babies to sell. Some children went to parents unable adopt in conventional ways for very high profits. Others went worse places, much worse places … Lilly felt as if she was going to be sick as she read through the details on how vile this woman was.

Girls who had second thoughts about the arrangement would be found overdosed in some gutter or fleabag hotel. Lilly's stomach turned again. Humans selling other humans struck an especially harsh chord inside of her. She hoped this one would be tortured a long time before she was killed.

"Lilly?" Vivienne placed her hand onto Lilly's shoulder after calling to her for the third time.

Lilly snapped her head up, jaw clenched tight, veins popping out of her neck. Her lips curled into a snarl revealing her descended canis, and she realized she was shaking.

"What?!" she spat before realizing it was Vivienne beside her.

Lilly's jaw unclenched as her eyes widened when she retracted her teeth, softening her features. "Sorry, Viv."

"I see you got the alert," Vivienne said cautiously lowering her hand.

"Yeah." Lilly was still a little snippy. She folded the TAC placing it back in her pocket as she got up. "I need a drink."

Lilly pushed past Vivienne into the hallway. Vivienne followed her down to the main living space where the bar was. Lilly grabbed a bottle of vodka off the bar with one glass. She poured it full to the rim, downed it and poured another. Lilly then walked over to the sofa and leaned against the back of it looking out the window.

Vivienne didn't want to push her. Something about this abduction was hard for Lilly. Vivienne went to the bar and poured herself a glass of wine, then leaned against the sofa beside Lilly. She could wait.

Lilly drank another glass and refilled it again. "I fucking hate humans. They are so horrible to each other. They do the most horrific things for money. They think everything they touch belongs to them. They destroy everything around them, and they call us monsters."

"They're not all like that, Lilly," Vivienne said slowly, watching her.

"All the ones in my experience were." Lilly took another hefty swig.

"I'm not sure what to say about that."

"That's a new experience for you, isn't it, Viv?" Lilly answered, wryly.

"I don't know what climbed up your ass, but you don't get to take it out on me. I haven't done shit to you!" Vivienne poked Lilly in the chest. "As a matter of fact, I've done more for you than you know. I don't need you to be grateful. I don't need you to think you owe me anything because I don't want anything from you. What you do need to do is stop being such an asshole. I'm not your enemy."

Vivienne snatched the glass of vodka out of Lilly's hand, downed the remainder of the liquid and pushed it back at her.

Lilly was stunned by the uncontrolled outburst. "Well, I'm not sure what to say about that." She mirrored Vivienne's words, breaking the tension of the moment.

"New experience for you?" Vivienne threw Lilly's words back with a smirk.

"Yeah," Lilly peered down at her shoes. Her posture slumped.

"What's got your panties twisted?"

"I did not expect such vulgarity from you, Viv," Lilly perked up.

"I haven't always been so prim and proper," Vivienne popped her eyebrows, smiling back softly.

"Seems you're full of surprises. Why are you so interested in me?"

"I find myself drawn to broken things. Maybe because I was broken once. You're not a bad person, Lilly. I think you've seen some really shitty things in your life. It's made your view a little dark." Vivienne sighed and took a sip of her wine, washing away the taste of vodka.

Lilly nodded and then refilled her glass half-way taking a sip. "I guess I have. You'd have a pretty dark view of life too if your father had sold you into slavery when you were a child. Then, after years of abuse, you were tortured to the point you wished you could die. If some unknown vampire stumbled over your lifeless body and turned you while you were unconscious, leaving before you woke up. You were left to wander the countryside starving and alone, not knowing what you were or what to do. I have always been on my own. I don't fit in anywhere, Viv. I didn't then and I don't now. Not in the human world. Not in this world. I only have myself. And I don't always like the company."

"That explains why you were so disturbed by this latest woman's disappearance."

"I want her to be dead. I want her tortured to death in the most extreme ways. I know that's a horrible thought. It makes me no better than they are. I can't help it. It's what I want," Lilly's sullen expression saddened Vivienne.

"One way or another, it'll all be over soon. I know you think you don't belong down here. You're right, you don't. You belong up there with us. You saw how it was in the facility. Everyone wants what's best for the whole community. We have a bond, a way to move forward. I'll make you a promise. When it's time to go, whether we've found whoever wanted the list or not, I'll take you to Rasa myself. Deal?" Viv extended her free hand.

Lilly was conflicted. She didn't like living amongst humans, looking over her shoulder all the time, never being able to trust anyone. There was no guarantee it would be any different up there. She had no choice except to take the leap. At least up there, she had a chance. If she didn't like Rasa, she would have access to a whole universe. She tucked her glass into the crook of her arm, grabbing Vivienne's hand, "I'll give it a shot. No promises though. I won't guarantee I'll stick around."

"Good enough."

Lilly let go of Vivienne's hand and lifted her glass back out of her arm. She then reached over clinking it with Vivienne's wine glass before they both drank. Vivienne left the room to discuss some community business with Vito as Lilly wandered back up to her room, hauling what remained of the vodka bottle with her. She had a book waiting for her to lose herself in.

When Lilly's eyes opened, the room was dark. She was in the reading chair, her book on the floor beside her. Her neck was crooked over in an awkward, uncomfortable position. She wasn't alone. Her head was being pressed into the chair, exposing her neck. She felt a stinging sensation in the side of her throat. Her heart raced, her vision blurred, her head became too heavy to lift. She tried to speak only to slur incoherently. Her tongue felt swollen, too big for her mouth. She couldn't scream, she couldn't run, she couldn't move on her own. Her body felt like it was floating, and the ceiling moved over her eyes. Lilly could see shadows beyond her view. Then the overhead light fixture became smaller, farther away. She was flailing, falling deep into the floor, through the kitchen below, through the basement as if a hole opened deep inside the earth to swallow her. Panic rose from her stomach into her chest. She tried to scream, she tried to grab onto something, anything. She was helpless. This was how her end would come.

'Thud.' Lilly snapped up in a panic. The book she had been reading fell off the arm of the chair onto the floor. She was terrified, sweating, breathing heavily. It was morning. She was still in the chair, in her room, by herself. It had all been a nightmare. There was no one with her. She hadn't been drugged or abducted. The stabbing in her neck was the sharp point of her own earring. She leaned forward, elbows on her knees, head in her hands until her breathing slowed.

It was strange how she could sleep like a baby with loud music vibrating through her chest, shouting, and horns honking. It was the quiet places like this that brought out her nightmares. The nightmare of being dragged out of her bed and tossed into a deep, dark pit. The terror in her mind of unimaginable tortures seeped to the surface as soon as she fell asleep. Lilly thought she had officially gone stir crazy. She had to get out for a while. She needed more noise than cackling chickens and whipping wind.

Lilly grabbed the glass off the table next to her, downing the last half-inch of vodka. The bottle was empty. She glanced at herself in the mirror on her way to the shower. She looked like crap. Her roots were grown out, her ends were frizzed, and she needed her eyebrows waxed. Actually, she needed everything waxed. Would it be too much to hope that this little town had a decent salon? One with an opening was an even bigger ask. Finding more colors than red and blond would certainly be a stretch. It was also time to stop waiting around. If she was supposed to be bait, she needed to be seen and this was as good a time as any to see what would shake out. It was time for her to go to town. She was finished playing the waiting game.

After a hot, relaxing shower Lilly slipped on a pair of jeans and the gray impact resistant shirt Ruzzio had given her. She grabbed her pink and gray hiking boots by the strings, threw them over her shoulder, and grasped her jacket in the same hand. On the way out to the hall, she picked up the vodka bottle and glass, and headed down the stairs. The glass was dropped off at the kitchen sink, the bottle in the recycling bin next to it. Her next goal was to find Vito somewhere on the property. Lilly pulled a pink and black knit cap out of her jacket pocket and placed it over her wet hair. She slipped into her jacket, then sat on the bench beside the back door to lace up her boots. While she was leaning over tying her laces, one of the house cats started pawing at them making it impossible to complete the task.

"Stop it, Maybelle." Lilly gently pushed the cat away.

Maybelle wasn't having any of it. The second Lilly had cleared her paws from the laces, she was right back into them. The push and pull went on for several minutes until Lilly gave in, picking the cat up to pet her. Maybelle purred and pressed her head under Lilly's chin. Once Maybelle was finished absorbing the amount of attention she wanted, she jumped out of Lilly's arms and slunk off down the hall. As she sat there watching the cat, a thought came to her. She hadn't considered herself a cat person as much as she considered her own personality like that of a cat's. Go where you want; get the attention you want and move on. Stay around for the food and occasional pat on the head before resuming your own agenda. She didn't stick around long enough for anyone to get tired of her. She always parted on good terms. It was more of a 'get along until you got along' lifestyle and it worked for her. She certainly wasn't a dog. There hadn't, up to this point, been a loyal bone in her body.

Is this what today was about? Lilly wondered to herself. The nightmare, the need to get out amongst people. Was it the urge to run before they could get rid of her? She shook off the thought as she opened the back door stepping into the cold. The wind felt good against her face. It wasn't the sharp, brisk, dry-cold wind it had been over most of the winter. It had changed to a damp, warmer than the air temperature kind of wind. The kind that came in the very early days of spring when the snow melted into the thawing mud, mixing into a gray slushy mess. She was relieved to be outside, away from the confinement of where her nightmare had held her.

Lilly took a deep breath. It was full of all the normal scents of melting snow, mud, and chicken shit. Further smells of the domiciles around the perimeter wafted toward her. She turned toward the side of the house, toward voices, crackling fire and the smell of smoke.

When she made her way around the corner, she saw Vito, Alonzo and one of the women whose name she could never remember clearing a patch of ground. They burned brush and dried up remnants of a long-forgotten vegetable garden. Vito was pulling out huge stones that were once a low boundary wall. He pitched them with the ease of skipping stones over a pond. A few hundred kilos were nothing for their kind.

"Morning," Lilly greeted the others.

Vito turned toward her, pitching another stone over his shoulder. "Ahh, Lilly. Nice to see you outside. Come to help clear the garden?"

"Well, actually, it's time to take a trip into town. I desperately need a haircut and a few other things."

"Shouldn't be too difficult to arrange a trip. I'll let the security detail in the town know to keep an eye out for you," Vito replied pulling out his phone.

"Make sure a couple of them stick out, but not too much. Don't want our mystery stalker to think we're expecting them if they see me today. We just want them to think we're on a normal amount of alert," Lilly instructed.

"Take Alonzo with you. It will look less conspicuous. Don't want anyone to think we'd let you travel alone," Vito pointed toward an overly excited Alonzo, who appeared happy for the reprieve from manual labor.

Lilly looked up at Vito with a mixture of indignation and annoyance before realizing what her face must have looked like. She quickly adjusted it to appear more concerned. "I can go myself. You look busy."

Vito belted out a hearty laugh. "Take him. Your Italian isn't very good. And besides, if you get into any trouble, he screams like a little girl," Vito laughed again.

Alonzo looked embarrassed. "It's true. I can scream a much lout," he smiled widely through his thick accent.

Lilly gave in. If taking Alonzo was the price she had to pay for a day out, it was worth it. "You're right. It's very nice of you to let him out of his work to take me, Vito. You wouldn't happen to know a good place for a haircut, would you?"

The woman, whose name Lilly had forgotten answered, "Alonzo can take you to the day spa at the end of the old train station. They can do anything you need."

"Waxing?" Lilly asked.

"Yes. They do waxing, nails, hair. Anything you want. It's not tourist season yet, so they won't be busy. Do you have euros? You shouldn't use a card." She paused. "Mmm, and use a different name too," she said shaking her finger as she nodded.

"Yes, I have euros. Thank you." Lilly nodded back.

Alonzo ran into the house to wash up and grab the truck keys while Lilly waited, taking in the pleasantness of being outside. He ran back out a short time later. Lilly thought to herself, she'd never seen the boy walk. He was without a doubt a dog: loyal to a fault, with all the excitement of a new puppy and all the refinement of one too. He would stay behind on Earth, not because he was afraid to go with the others, but because he was loyal to his family, and they were staying behind. It was a shame he would miss out on what the universe had to offer a curious young man like him. She lagged a little as they approached the truck. She had done so much traveling she couldn't remember which side she should get in on, so she let him approach first. He opened the passenger door for her, which she hadn't expected, and waited for her to get in before closing it. He took the driver's side, and they were off.

The drive through town was uneventful. There were a couple dozen townies and three or four that were obviously her security team. Aside from the difference in their scents, they didn't all blend in flawlessly, which was what she wanted. Lilly wasn't sure if it was obvious to everyone or if she had merely gotten used to picking up on outliers.

Most of the shops were open with a few that looked interesting. The art store was someplace she would visit for sure. Two clothing stores, a bookshop and a one stop shop caught her eye. The parking lot was close to empty when they turned in with seven cars in a space having the capacity of thirty.

By the time she unfastened her seatbelt, Alonzo was already out and had opened her door. Jeez, he was working hard for her approval.

"Thanks," Lilly said, sliding off the seat onto the ground two feet below her.

Alonzo bowed extending his arm toward the building. "So, Lilly, what do you want first to do?"

"Uh, I guess a haircut and color," she shrugged.

"Okay. After you."

They entered the building. Lilly decided at first glance it was a tourist trap. Patrons had to walk past tons of products displayed on shelves to get to the reception desk. Heaps of designer hair products, flat irons, blow dryers, clothes, scarves, and an array of gaudy jewelry. Four stylists and two nail technicians sat in their chairs reading the latest magazines and chatting amongst themselves. An older woman closest to the reception desk quickly rose as the bell over the door chimed when they entered. Lilly only saw one other customer in the shop, and she smelled … odd. The employees were all human, but she wasn't sure what the customer was. She smelled familiar and unfamiliar at the same time. Something about her was off, making Lilly suspicious of her being the person who wanted the list. Lilly caught Alonzo look intently at the woman.

"Stop staring," she whispered, as she pretended to look at a hair mask.

"The woman. She's one of them. An Acer," he whispered back.

"Acer?" Then it dawned on her. She smelled a lot like the man in the hallway, Erik. "Æsir," Lilly corrected. She wasn't sure why she had expected the entire security team to be vampires. There was no reason why she should have.

"Ahh. Æsir. Bene," he nodded.

Lilly sighed. "Come on."

They approached the reception desk.

"How may I help you?" the woman said in Italian.

Lilly was formulating the proper reply in her head when Alonzo responded to the woman in their native tongue.

"My friend would like a haircut and a color."

"Does your friend not speak Italian?" the woman asked, looking at Lilly smugly.

"I understand better than I speak," Lilly replied, also in Italian.

The woman smiled at her, "What language is easier for you?"

"I am fluent in French, Spanish, Portuguese, German, Dutch, Mandarin, English and a few others," Lilly smiled back.

"Oh," the woman's smirk dropped from her face. "Excuse me." She turned to the other women in the room.

Lilly thought for a spa that catered to tourists, she seemed a little snotty. A younger woman, mid-twenties hopped up with a big smile greeting Lilly in Spanish. She took Lilly by the arm and led her back to her chair.

"Good morning, I'm Bella. What color are you looking for today? Don't worry, none of these old bags speak Spanish," she giggled.

Thank God, Lilly thought. Spanish was one of her best languages. She didn't need Alonzo to interpret anything. At least this girl was young. "Good! I'm Maybelle. You can call me May. Cut it short in the back, long in the front so I can braid it and pull it up into a knot. Black all over with blue highlights. That ought to freak them out, don't you think?"

Bella pulled Lilly back into her chair and produced a barber cape from her drawer flinging it around Lilly. "Perfect! This is going to be fun."

Over the next three hours, Lilly was cut, colored, manicured and waxed to perfection. The Æsir woman had left and a string of male vampires had come and gone receiving haircuts and shaves. Two female vampires came in together for mani-pedis, remaining until Lilly was finished. Poor Alonzo sat and waited the entire time, fidgeting uncontrollably.

Lilly was pleased with the entire experience and tipped Bella very well. The older women exuded mixed feelings of both jealousy over the tip and mortification over Lilly's new look. Lilly and Alonzo spent the rest of the day shopping, only stopping to eat, and getting back to the villa a little before dark. Alonzo helped Lilly carry her bags up to her room. She was sorting through her finds of the day when her smart watch buzzed. She had a message, an encrypted message, which meant her friend was back.

She tossed the bag in her hand onto the bed and pulled out her laptop. She opened the tor browser, navigating to her secure message center and entered her decryption key. The message window popped up.

"About fucking time," she said out loud.

Nice hair. Too bad you've hidden away all this time, like a scared little mouse. Goodbye Lilly.

That was it. That was all the message said. This asshole was taunting her by keeping her a silent hostage all this time, and now what? It was over? Whoever sent it knew who she was, where she was and what she looked like. They had probably known the entire time she had been here. She stared at the screen for a moment before calling Vivienne.

CHAPTER SIX

Vivienne paced in front of the fireplace, biting into the skin on the side of her fingernail as she watched Ruzzio work on Lilly's laptop while Harmon peered over his shoulder. Lilly stood beside him watching nervously. Vito and the others were positioned around the periphery of the room with security teams patrolling the grounds. Everyone was on high alert.

"Well?" Vivienne asked anxiously.

"Ida isn't configured for this," Ruzzio replied, with frustration.

"We should try it." Harmon urged.

"It's not ready!" Ruzzio snapped back.

"What's not ready?" Vivienne's patience was waning.

"A new program we've been working on. We haven't tested it live, and the integrations aren't set up for Ida yet. It probably won't even work for this application." Ruzzio sounded impatient.

"But it might," Vivienne said, sternly.

"It could," Harmon replied, hopefully.

Ruzzio scoffed. "Maybe with a few more weeks of testing, and we would need to take the laptop back to Rasa."

"No. That laptop cannot be taken into the heart of the community. It's too big of a risk if there's any way at all it could be tracked back there. You need to make it work here," Vivienne demanded.

"What if we take it to the Montana facility? It's nearly empty now, isn't it? Don't they have everything there that Rasa has?" Lilly asked.

"Only the top floor is still occupied. They're mostly using it to transport out. They have everything we need in the lab, but it'll still take time," Ruzzio answered.

"We don't have time!" Vivienne scolded. "We now know they traced Lilly here. We expected that. What we didn't expect was not a single one of us sensed them. We also have to assume they know who and what she is and have already figured out who everyone living here is. That wasn't entirely unexpected either, but we thought we'd have gained information about them in the process. We need to do everything necessary to find out who they are."

"If there is even a remote chance, they are tracking this laptop, probability is they will follow it back to the facility. We have a better chance of finding them if we can get Sadie working. And the only place we can do that here, is at the facility," Harmon said.

"Sadie? Who is Sadie?" Vivienne asked, leveling exasperation at Harmon.

"Sadie isn't a who, Sadie is a what. Secure Automated Digital Interface Enhancement, SADIE," Ruzzio said, and turned to face her.

Vivienne sighed. "Let me warn Ben we're coming. He's the last person I want caught with his pants down. His temper has been bad enough lately without blindsiding him.

Vivienne went into the other room to make the call. When she came back, she looked irritated.

"He said to give him half an hour. We need to port to the shack and go in from there."

"The shack?" Ruzzio asked. "Why?"

"Because they're locking down the facility. Just pack the laptop," Vivienne snapped.

Ruzzio complied before checking to make sure the Villa's surveillance and intrusion monitors were set. Thirty minutes later, they ported to the shack.

The dilapidated building was exactly how Lilly had pictured it. Dusty, old and smelling of dead animals. Everything was covered in cobwebs. Only four of them had come. Vivienne, Lilly, Ruzzio and Harmon. Harmon placed his hand on the back wall of the shack revealing the entrance to the facility and waited for the guard to buzz them in. At the end of the hall, they stepped into an elevator making their way down to level six. They were met by two Jur sentinels, cleared and allowed to continue to Ruzzio and Harmon's old lab. It had been closed for over a month when they transferred the staff to Rasa. Inside, the lab was just a square, white room void of any furnishings.

Ruzzio motioned everyone to the center of the room. "Ida, set lab seven, download Sadie to the sandbox."

The room transformed itself into a proper workspace. Counters and stools appeared out of the walls. Viewing screens and two comfortable lounge chairs pushed down from the ceiling and up from the floor, along with a small table and two straight-back metal chairs.

"Grab a seat ladies, this is going to take a while," Ruzzio said pulling Lilly's laptop out of the bag.

Vivienne and Lilly sat at the small table; Lilly in the corner slouching against the wall, Vivienne across from her. Vivienne pulled out her TAC and began looking at wedding stuff, leaving Lilly with nothing to do. Lilly sat as long as she could, before getting up to watch what Ruzzio was doing. The interface was like nothing she was the least bit familiar with, but it didn't take her long to start figuring out the connections. She watched quietly as code flew over the screens before Ruzzio told her Sadie was ready to start. He connected her laptop. All that was left to do was wait. They watched as Sadie evaluated every single keystroke Lilly had ever made on the keyboard. Every location she had been to and every tor and browser connection she had made was processed and categorized.

Four hours later a female voice, thicker and more sultry than Ida's began to speak. "Evaluation complete. Analysis shows the profile belonging to user 'Aurer' origination point tracking."

A bar appeared on the bottom of the three-dimensional display cycling through a series of zeroes and ones, several times. They watched and waited. A model of the earth appeared on the display. It rotated backward and forward dozens of times before looking outward into space. Sadie marked numerous points in the vicinity of the planet with activity dates for the user. Analysis complete.

"That doesn't make any sense," Lilly said.

"Yes, it does," Vivienne said from behind her. "Ruzzio, have Sadie run a comparison of the location of all community members against the active times and dates."

"Sadie, run analysis," Ruzzio commanded.

"You think it's someone in the community?" Lilly asked.

"No, it's for elimination," Harmon answered.

"If it's not someone in the community ..." Lilly began.

"… then it's someone else capable of being in space," Harmon finished her thought.

"We just need proof to give to Ivan," Vivienne said.

"Analysis complete. Results show no correlation of any community members with any active times for user 'Aurer,'" Sadie announced.

"Ruzzio, do we have a way to track any personnel on the Council?" Vivienne asked.

"Only the ones who have been in the facility. Everyone who enters is passively scanned. Sadie, run analysis against all known Council personnel," Ruzzio commanded.

"What is the Council?" Lilly asked.

"Council of the Divine. They're the authority in The Everything. They've begrudgingly been assisting us with moving to Rasa, but there are many who are vocal about our immaturity as a species. They don't think we should be mixing with the Æsir or any other advanced species for that matter. It's all a big power game to them," Harmon answered. He was very anti-political.

They watched the display for a few minutes longer.

"Analysis complete. Results show no correlation of any known Council members with any active times for user 'Aurer,'" Sadie announced.

"Shit," Vivienne responded. "Now that, Lilly, is a dead end."

"What do we do now?" Lilly asked.

"There's not much we can do. Turn over the information to Ivan and let him deal with it. Reinforce our security as much as possible and continue doing what we're doing until they make another move. *If* they make another move." Vivienne answered.

"We can't just give up." Lilly was angry.

"What do you expect us to do? At least now we know someone or a group of someones are out there watching us, trying to figure out who every one of us is. They wanted that list so they could find out who was moving, who was staying and family ties from what I can best figure. We have no way to find them out there. So, tell me. What do you expect us to do?" Vivienne was just as frustrated as the rest of them. But her job was done. She was done. She had other things to do. She was handing all of this over and shutting it down.

Lilly stood there staring at her with her mouth open. Ruzzio and Harmon recorded the data and sent it to Vivienne's TAC before turning Sadie off and resetting the room.

"Let's go," Vivienne said, after checking her TAC.

"Go where?" Lilly asked angrily.

Vivienne turned on Lilly. "You are going back to the vineyard until I can get you up to Rasa. They," she pointed to Ruzzio and Harmon, "are going back to wherever they came from, and I am going home to plan my daughter's ceremonies! Now get your ass moving!"

Lilly bit her tongue hard swallowing down bitterness and resentment. For the first time in her life, she decided to stay quiet. She decided she wouldn't let her own temper or ego fuck this up for her. She was going to Rasa.

She followed Vivienne out to the shack and back to the vineyard. She was angry, but she wasn't stupid. She let Ruzzio destroy her laptop. In her mind, she wouldn't be needing it again. It was useless to her.

The second she got back to the vineyard, Lilly grabbed a fresh bottle of vodka, went straight to her room, crushed her watch so she wouldn't get any more alerts and started painting. Her part was over. It was just another thing she would need to leave behind her and move on.

Two weeks later, Vivienne kept her promise. Lilly was on her way to Rasa. She stood in the port line waiting her turn to step into a new life in another world. She exited the other side of the port into a hallway with a total of eight ports, four on each side. Her group was taken through the hallway into the great hall of the Community Center. Everything was sleek, pristine, and utterly devoid of anything remotely resembling decoration.

Orientation for her group lasted a little over two hours. She was assigned a studio flat and a workspace. The apartment was a blank canvas like the rest of the newly constructed city. Vivienne had gotten her a job on the design team. She would be adding the things that would make the community spaces welcoming for everyone. The team would also be tasked with designing the interiors of the living spaces. It was the perfect job for Lilly. Creating. She welcomed the challenge. The best part was that she would be working on her own with a team of service units under her command. No one would force her to socialize. She would get specifics from the residents, create their spaces, and leave without ever seeing anyone. Public spaces would have groups working on them, but most of the other designers were like she was, independent and introverted, not wanting to indulge in frivolous conversation.

Even the most flamboyant designers preferred their own company and ordering their service units around. As she walked into her assigned workspace for the first time, she found Vivienne had brought in all her art from the Amsterdam loft. Every painting and digital image was there, every sketchbook, every paintbrush. All of it was there. She would spread her art throughout public spaces, to be seen by the entire community and only Vivienne and Violet would know it was hers. It would be their secret. For the first time in her nine hundred years, she felt like she had a place she could belong. She felt satisfied.

ALSO BY

JOYCE SERRANO

THE TURNED GODS SERIES

Original Grace - Book 1
Immortals in the Everything - Book 2

THE TURNED GODS - CHARACTER COMPANION SERIES

Galin's Alley
Lilly's Game